For Catherine – M.H.
For Zoë – B.W.

Celebrity Cat copyright © Frances Lincoln Limited 2006
Text copyright © Meredith Hooper 2006
Illustrations copyright © Bee Willey 2006
The right of Meredith Hooper to be identified
as the author of this work has been asserted by her in accordance
with the Copyright, Designs and Patents Act, 1988 (United Kingdom).

PHOTOGRAPHIC ACKNOWLEDGEMENTS
Please note: the pages in this book are not numbered. The story begins on page 6.
For permission to reproduce the paintings on the following pages
and for supplying photographs, the Publishers would like to thank:
Louvre, Paris/www.bridgeman.co.uk: page 28 & 37 (bottom right)
The Metropolitan Museum of Art, Rogers Fund, 1919 (19.164)
Photo © 1998 The Metropolitan Museum of Art: page 20 & 37 (top right)
© National Gallery, London: page 12 (left) & 36 (top),
page 12 (right) & 36 (bottom), page 13 & 37 (top left)
Prado, Madrid/www.bridgeman.co.uk: page 25 & 37 (bottom left)

First published in Great Britain and in the USA in 2006 by
Frances Lincoln Children's Books, 4 Torriano Mews
Torriano Avenue, London NW5 2RZ
www.franceslincoln.com

Distributed in the USA by Publishers Group West

British Library Cataloguing in Publication Data
available on request

ISBN 10:1-84507-290-1
ISBN 13:978-1-84507-290-2

Illustrated in pencil, oil pastels, acrylic and Photoshop 7

Printed in China
1 3 5 7 9 8 6 4 2

Celebrity Cat

Meredith Hooper

Illustrated by *Bee Willey*

FRANCES LINCOLN CHILDREN'S BOOKS

All over the city, cats were gathering –
fat cats, skinny cats, bold cats, bad cats,
sleek and shabby, striped and tabby.

In twos and threes, and ones and twos,
the cats crept and hid, jumped and slid.
Down by the river, in the busy dark,
the clock began striking midnight.
It was Cats' Visiting Night at the art gallery
and all the cats were coming.

Everywhere the cats looked in the art gallery,
they saw paintings of dogs, and horses,
and birds. There were paintings with lions
and tigers, even monkeys. But there were
almost NO paintings with cats.

The cats were cross.
"It isn't right, it isn't fair," they hissed.

Felissima Cat stared at a painting of a chair. Everyone knew that the chair belonged to a well-known artistic cat who sat in it for hours.

Where was the cat?

As for the painting of a house where three friendly cats lived – not one of them could be seen!

Felissima Cat padded past a painting of a tiger in a storm. How ridiculous, sniffed Felissima, when it could be, should be, a cat!

Felissima walked home through
the dark streets, thinking hard.
She climbed the winding stairs to her room
behind the chimney-pots where she worked.

Felissima Cat prepared her paintbrushes.
She squeezed the colours out of the little
tubes of paint. She put on her painting apron
and began a new picture.

It was Cats' Visiting Night in the art gallery
again. Everyone was there.
City cats, pretty cats, stray cats, alley cats,
cats with their families,
cats from park benches,
growl cats, prowl cats.

Felissima stood, excited and proud,
in front of a velvet curtain.

"Friends," said the Chief of All Cats,
"tonight we have a real treat.
Felissima has painted some
very special new pictures for us."

The curtain opened.
"Oh," cried the cats, "look, look!
At last!"

"Felissima Cat," said the Chief of All Cats,
"for too long we have been left out of paintings.
You and I will travel the world. Everyone must
see how important we cats really are."

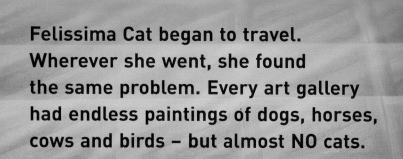

Felissima Cat began to travel.
Wherever she went, she found
the same problem. Every art gallery
had endless paintings of dogs, horses,
cows and birds – but almost NO cats.

In New York, Felissima noticed that
the cats had been left out in the picture
of people having a picnic. How silly!
she thought. Cats are ALWAYS busy
at harvest time.

Felissima painted a new picture.
She put one cat chasing mice and one in the tree.

The cats of New York took Felissima
to the best restaurants. She partied
all night. Felissima was famous.
She was a Celebrity Cat.

In Madrid, Felissima saw at once that the cat
was missing in the painting of a dog and people staring.
It was obvious that they were all staring at a cat,
but the cat had been left out.

Felissima's new painting added
the missing cat, washing her whiskers.

The cats of Madrid were ecstatic.
"Bravo!" they shouted.

Twelve of the most handsome Spanish cats
serenaded Felissima in a midnight concert.
She signed autographs until her paw ached.

In Paris, Felissima admired
a beautiful painting of a lady.
As soon as she saw her,
Felissima knew why the lady
was smiling.

So Felissima created her own
masterpiece, *Lady with a Cat*.
Cats queued for hours to see
Felissima's painting.

But Felissima was becoming weary of the crowds and the photographs. She was tired of being a Celebrity Cat. She longed to be private, to be a cat nobody knew. She missed her own little room in London, behind the chimney pots. It was time to go home.

It was Cats' Visiting Night at the art gallery again.
Down by the river, in the busy dark,
the clock began striking midnight.
All over the city cats were gathering –
rooftop cats and bin-bag cats,
hard cats and comfy cats,
hopeful cats and lonely cats.

"Tonight," said the Chief of All Cats,
"our own dear Felissima, Celebrity Cat,
is making a star appearance.
We cannot wait to see what she has
painted for us this time."

The velvet curtain drew back.
The crowd of cats gasped in astonishment.
There was NO painting!

Felissima quietly stroked her small paws.

"My friends," said Felissima,
"you may be wondering why
I have not painted a picture for you.
I have travelled the world – and truly,
there are not enough paintings with cats.
But now I understand why.
We cats have not been left out of paintings.
WE HAVE CHOSEN NOT TO BE IN THEM.
Perhaps we haven't arrived yet,
or we have gone somewhere else.
Perhaps we are there, but we can't be seen.
We cats go where we want to go.
We do what we want to do.
Because we are cats."

Felissima walked home alone
through the dark streets.
She climbed the winding stairs to her room
behind the chimney-pots.

Felissima prepared her paintbrushes and squeezed
the colours out of the little tubes of paint.
Then she found her self-portrait,
Cat with Half-eaten Fish.
And, tail twitching with concentration,
she began to paint.

Look at a collection of paintings and you won't find many with cats. Sometimes there's a cat in the kitchen, or sitting on a girl's lap, or staring at a bird, but usually the cats look as if they are just pausing, on the way to somewhere else. So every time cats visit an art gallery for Cats' Visiting Night they have to search very hard to see any paintings of themselves.

Felissima thought of some places in paintings where cats belonged. Perhaps you might like to find some more.

Van Gogh's Chair

◎ Felissima added a cat to *Van Gogh's Chair*, by Vincent van Gogh (born 1853–died 1890).

She added three cats to *The Courtyard of a House in Delft*, by Pieter de Hooch (born 1629–died 1684).

She replaced the tiger with a cat in *Tiger in a Tropical Storm (Surprised!)*, by Henri Rousseau (born 1844–died 1910).

These three paintings can be seen in The National Gallery, London.

◎ Felissima put two cats into *The Harvesters*, by Pieter Bruegel the Elder (active by 1551, died 1569). This painting can be seen in The Metropolitan Museum of Art, New York

◎ Felissima added a cat to *Las Meninas* or *The Family of Philip IV*, by Diego Velázquez (born 1599–died 1660). This painting can be seen in The Prado, Madrid.

◎ Felissima gave the Mona Lisa a cat to hold in *La Gioconda* or *Mona Lisa*, by Leonardo da Vinci (born 1452–died 1519). This painting can be seen in The Louvre, Paris.

The Courtyard of a House in Delft

Tiger in a Tropical Storm (Surprised!)

The Harvesters

Las Meninas or *The Family of Philip IV*

La Gioconda or *Mona Lisa*